The Shine Man

A Christmas Story

Written by
Mary Quattlebaum

Illustrated by
Tim Ladwig

Eerdmans Books for Young Readers

Grand Rapids, Michigan   Cambridge, U.K.

To Helen, a maker of spoolies, and to John and Caroline,
who bring lots of shine to Christmas.
— *M. Q.*

For Marvin Martin. He inspires many to give
by his own loving example.
— *T. L.*

Text © 2001 by Mary Quattlebaum
Illustrations © 2001 by Tim Ladwig

Published 2001 by Eerdmans Books for Young Readers
An imprint of Wm. B. Eerdmans Publishing Company
255 Jefferson S.E., Grand Rapids, Michigan 49503
P.O. Box 163, Cambridge, CB3 9PU U.K.
Printed in Hong Kong

01 02 03 04 05 06 07   7 6 5 4 3 2 1

Library of Congress Cataloging-in-Publication Data
Quattlebaum, Mary.
The shine man / written by Mary Quattlebaum; illustrated by Tim Ladwig.
p.cm.
Summary: During the hard times of 1932, a poor shoe shine man gives a child his cap,
gloves and an angel made from a spool, then receives a wonderful gift in return.
ISBN 0-8028-5181-9 (alk. paper)
[1. Shoe shiners — Fiction. 2. Generosity — Fiction. 3. Christmas — Fiction.
4. Depression — 1929 — Fiction.] I.Ladwig, Tim, ill. II. Title.
PZ7.Q19 Sh 2001
[E] — dc2
00-048370
The illustrations were painted in watercolor with acrylic medium
on texture made with brushed-on acrylic soft gel.
The display copy was hand-lettered by John Stevens.
The text type was set in Bernhard Modern.

Hear that rickety-rack of wheels over track? Hear the cry of the train? Oh, it takes me back to a tale my daddy would tell of the Christmas of '32.

Money was so tight then that gifts were few. In fact, many folks couldn't afford a decent house or food enough to fill their children's mouths. They lived in shacks the cold wind blew right through. They stood in line for bread. Some men left everything behind to look for work. They rode the rails from town to town, desperate to earn a dime.

Larry was one of these men. He had traveled so long that home was just another shack beside the tracks, so far that no one knew his name. Most folks called him Shine Man, on account of he polished shoes. Why, with just a rag and a bit of blacking, he could make the dingiest, dirtiest pair sparkle like new. Thing was, moving, moving, moving as he did, Larry had lost all interest in people. He only looked at shoes.

And that's how it was three days before Christmas, when Larry jumped off a train not far from here.

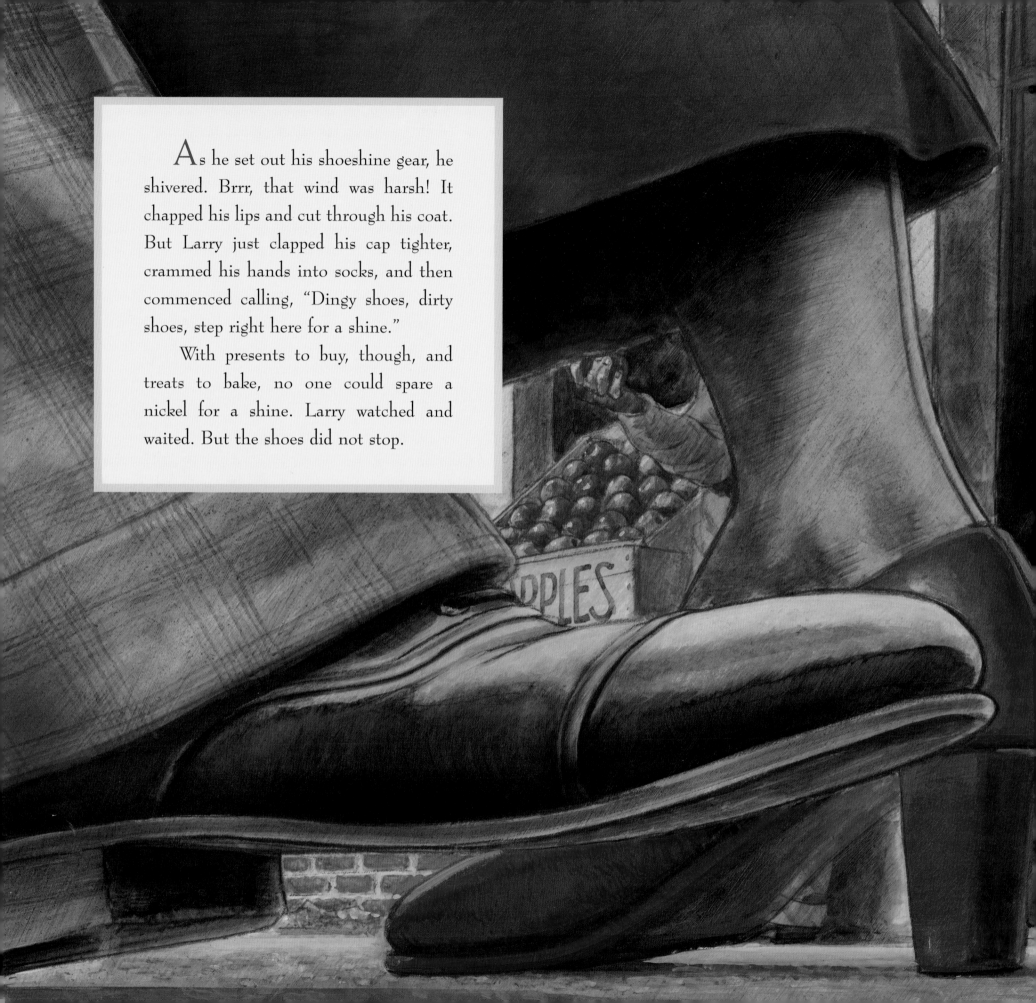

As he set out his shoeshine gear, he shivered. Brrr, that wind was harsh! It chapped his lips and cut through his coat. But Larry just clapped his cap tighter, crammed his hands into socks, and then commenced calling, "Dingy shoes, dirty shoes, step right here for a shine."

With presents to buy, though, and treats to bake, no one could spare a nickel for a shine. Larry watched and waited. But the shoes did not stop.

Then 'round about twilight, when the crowds had thinned, Larry noticed something on the sidewalk.

Just a bit of trash. A few empty spools and cloth scraps, a tuft of yarn. But Larry couldn't help staring. Their shape reminded him of something.

He set to threading and fixing, tucking and folding. As he worked, the shadows crept close as eager children. And before you could say "Good Christmas Morning," Larry gave one last smooth to the yarn.

"Hey, Shine Man," shrilled a kid's voice. "You got a doll baby there?"

Larry ignored the kid. "Would you look at that!" he said to himself, gazing at the tiny thing he had made. "It's a spoolie. I made me a Christmas angel."

"A spoolie?" asked the kid.

Larry tucked the little angel into his pocket. Funny how a bit of wood and string could call to mind . . . oh . . . tree-shine and pie-smell, the warmth of a fire, kind faces.

Then that shrill voice again: "I sure would like a spoolie."

For the first time, the Shine Man glanced at the kid. Or, rather, at his shoes.

And those shoes were pitiful. Cracked leather stuffed with cardboard. Twisted laces full of knots. Then as the boy bent to tug a droopy sock, Larry noticed his wind-tangled hair.

"Fah," snorted the Shine Man. "You don't need a spoolie, you need a cap. Running around in the cold — Boy, you'll catch your death."

"Don't got a cap," the boy mumbled.

"Too bad for you," said Larry, but as he turned away, the spoolie rattled. And before he knew what his own hand was doing, Larry had stripped off his cap, dusted it once, and shoved it on the kid's matted head.

"Don't look for more than that," he grumbled.

"Thanks!" The boy shuffled off.

The temperature dropped that night, and the sky filled with snow. The next morning the city glowed like a Christmas card.

But the wind was bitter for those working outside. Larry tried to shield his cold ears with his sock-gloves as he called, "Dingy shoes, dirty shoes, step right here for a shine."

But the busy shoes hurried by.

Except for one pair.

One pitiful pair.

And this evening — believe it or not — those poor shoes looked even worse.

"Boy," said Larry, "what happened to your laces?"

"Laces?" One shoe scuffed against the other. "I guess I gave them away."

"Gave them away?" Larry shrugged. "Then your feet will freeze. It's as simple as that. Laces help keep out the snow."

But the boy paid no mind to Larry's words.

"Hi, Spoolie," he said to the angel.

"Forget the spoolie," grumbled the Shine Man, "and think of your own cold feet. Not that I care, but where are your parents? You need some winter clothes."

"Times are hard," said the boy. "We're just getting by."

Larry nodded. He knew about just getting by.

"Where's your home?"

"I move around," said the boy, "but I know where I was born. Shine Man, I was born in a barn."

Larry knew about moving around, but a kid born in a barn — fah! "That sounds like a hard-luck story to me."

"It's the truth." The boy gave a solemn sniff. "And the barn was cold. Real cold."

Larry narrowed his eyes. "How do you know it was cold — you just being born?"

"I *know*." The kid shivered as he reached down to wipe the snow from his shoes.

And for the first time, the Shine Man noticed the boy's hands. Red, they were, and cracked with cold.

The wind struck. In Larry's pocket, the spoolie shook.

"Boy, you cause me nothing but trouble," the Shine Man grumbled, tugging off his sock-gloves and pulling them over the boy's hands. "Trouble and cold. Now, don't come bothering me tomorrow."

"But tomorrow's Christmas Eve!" The boy flapped one sock. "Bye, Spoolie," he said, and added, "Thank you, Shine Man."

"Fah" was Larry's only response.

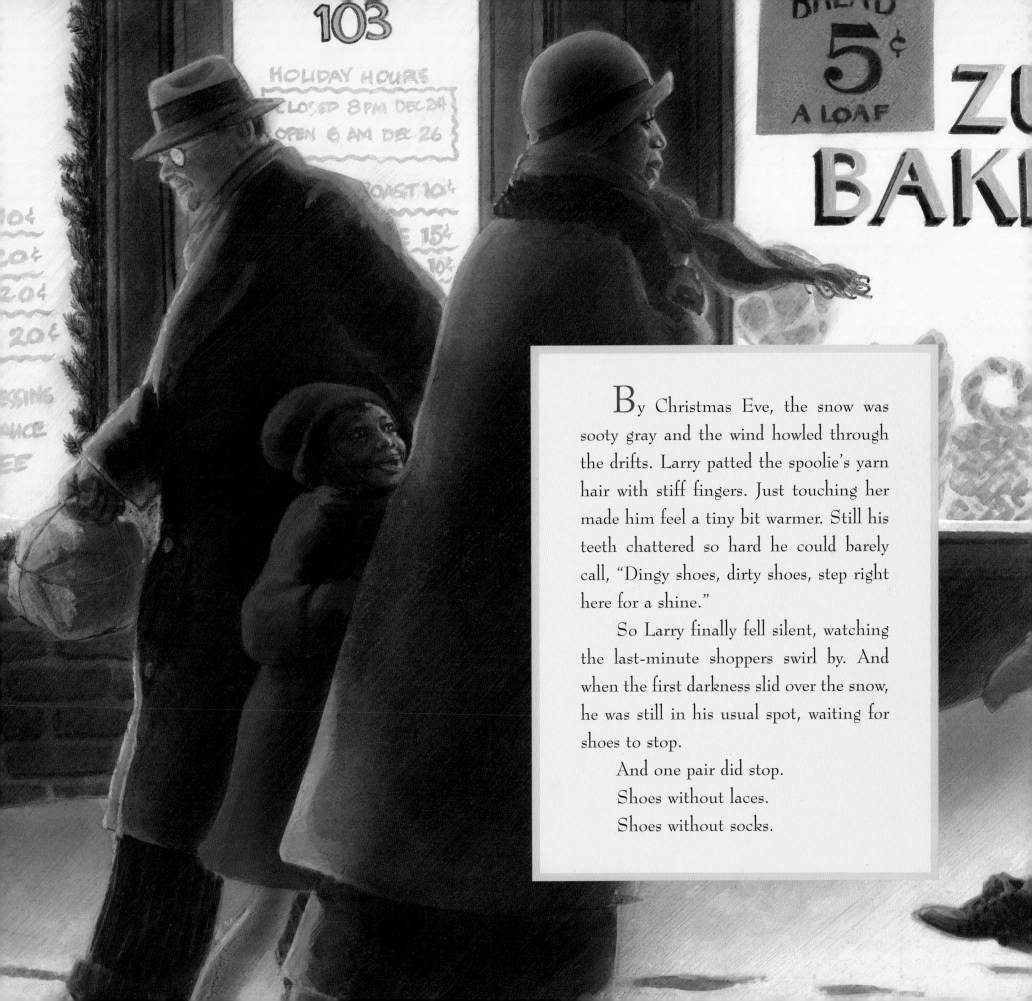

By Christmas Eve, the snow was sooty gray and the wind howled through the drifts. Larry patted the spoolie's yarn hair with stiff fingers. Just touching her made him feel a tiny bit warmer. Still his teeth chattered so hard he could barely call, "Dingy shoes, dirty shoes, step right here for a shine."

So Larry finally fell silent, watching the last-minute shoppers swirl by. And when the first darkness slid over the snow, he was still in his usual spot, waiting for shoes to stop.

And one pair did stop.
Shoes without laces.
Shoes without socks.

"Boy!" Larry almost fell over. "What did you do with your socks?"

The boy stood first on one foot, then on the other. His bare ankles stuck out.

"Socks?" He sneezed. "I guess I gave them away."

"Gave them away?" Larry sighed. "What fool gives his clothes away?"

The boy bowed and tipped his cap with one sock-glove. "I wonder," he said quietly, "what fool gives his clothes away." Then he asked, "How are you, Larry?"

The Shine Man stiffened and clenched his hands. "How do you know my name?"

The boy solemnly sniffed. "I told you, I just *know*."

"You heard someone call me."

"They yell 'Shine Man,'" said the boy.

"Fah." Larry dismissed the boy's words. "Well, I'm not such a knowing one as you, for your name doesn't trip off my tongue. Should I keep calling you 'Boy'?"

"You can call me anything." The voice came soft and low. "I'll answer."

Then the old shoes turned and shuffled away.

Shoes without laces. Shoes without socks.

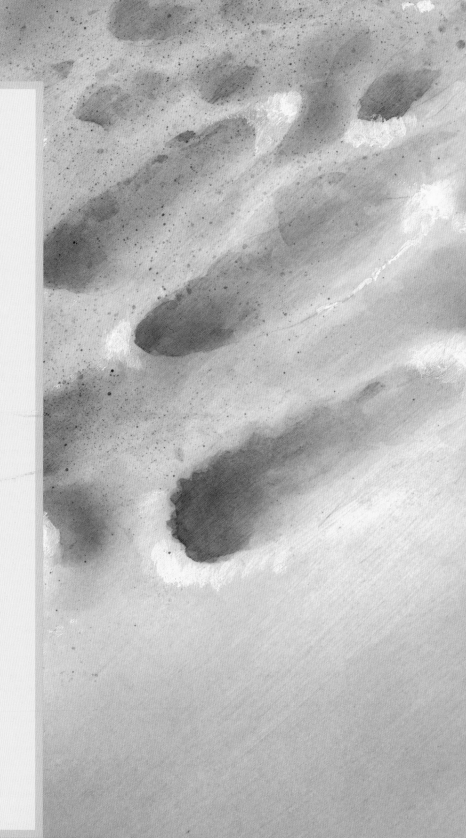

"Wait," Larry called, and as the shoes stopped and then slowly approached he added, almost kindly, "Boy, I bet you can tell me this. What's Santa bringing you this year?"

The boy said, "Maybe socks."

Socks! Larry shook his head. What kind of gift was socks? Warm, sure, but a kid should have something special.

The wind slapped him hard on the back, and he felt the spoolie shake.

For a moment, Larry watched the snow shift across the quiet street. Then he reached into his pocket and quickly lifted out the wings. He watched as the boy's big sock-gloves closed over the spoolie. Closed over his angel friend.

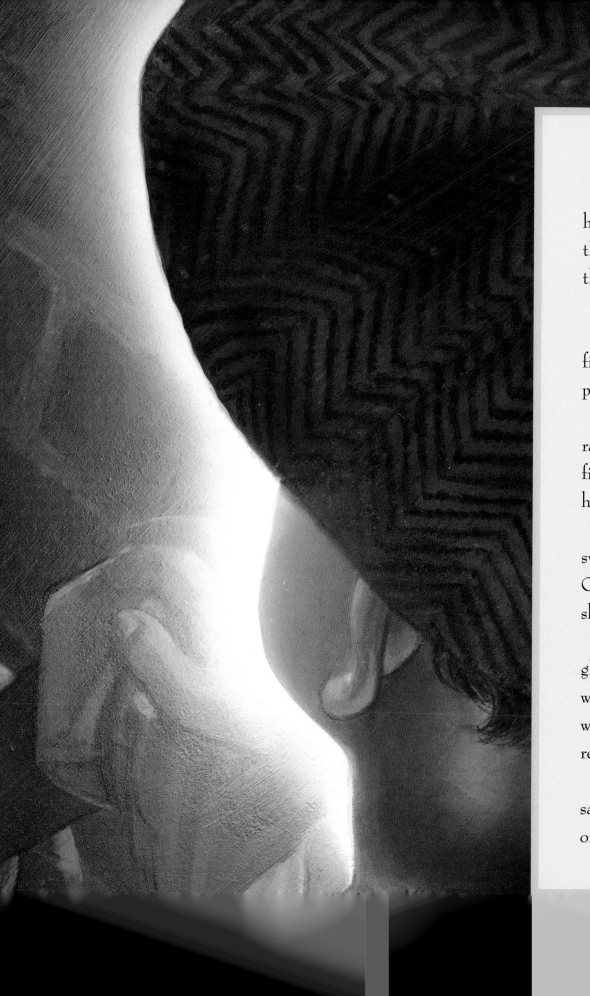

Suddenly Larry felt very cold.

"That's that," he said, letting his hand drop. "Now, don't go roughhousing that angel. She's not used to being thrown."

"Oh, no."

Larry cleared his throat, his gaze fixed on the snow. Those shoes, those pitiful shoes, were all he seemed to see.

"Boy," Larry briskly scooped up his rag, "I'm going to send you home with the finest Christmas shoes ever. Step right here for a shine."

And with that, Larry commenced to swoop and glide with his polishing cloth. Over those shoes, over and over those shoes. Again and again and again.

The shadows deepened and the snow glittered under the stars, and still Larry worked, on and on, until he saw what he wanted — a light, soft and white, reflected in those shoes.

And as he slowly lifted his head, to say "Merry Christmas" and send the child on his way, Larry gasped.

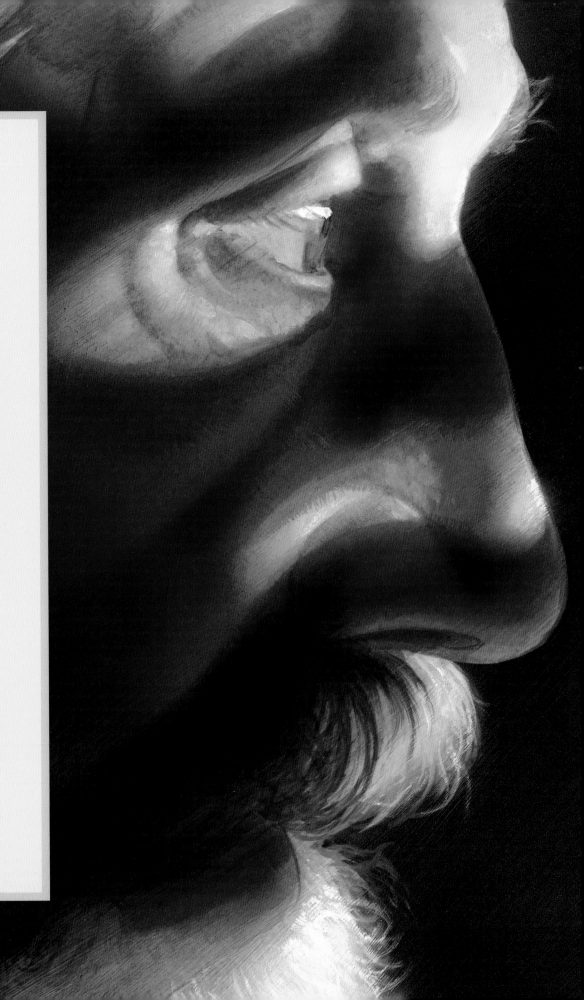

For the light came not from the street lamps, the stars, or the moon.

It shone from the face of the boy.

Softer than moon glow, warmer than sun kiss, brighter than new shoe shine.

The boy reached down to help Larry rise, and at his touch the chill that shook the Shine Man vanished. "Boy!" he cried out, shielding his eyes. "Please tell me who you are."

The boy faced Larry squarely. Light spilled from his cap to his shoes.

"Well," he said. "I guess you could say I am . . ." He grinned. "I guess you could call me . . ."

"You are the One." Larry trembled. "The Heavenly Child."

"So I've been called." The boy nodded. "But you could also call me" — that grin flashed again — "you could also call me . . . Shine Man."

"Shine Man!" Larry laughed. "Shine Man! Oh, you are, Boy, you are."

And then the boy laughed, too, and tightened his hold on Larry's hand.

Suddenly the Shine Man found himself looking down, down, down at the shacks, the sleeping streets. Larry saw the bare trees small as pins and the train tiny as a spool. Then he and the boy were swinging high, high, high up through the sky.

And all they did for the
rest of the night . . . was shine.